Cockadoodle-doo, Mr Sultana!

Other brilliant stories to collect:

Cockadoodle -doo, Mr Sultana!

Retold by
Michael Morpurgo

Illustrated by
Michael Foreman

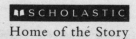
Home of thé Story

Scholastic Children's Books,
Commonwealth House, 1–19 New Oxford Street,
London WC1A 1NU, UK
a division of Scholastic Ltd
London ~ New York ~ Toronto ~ Sydney ~ Auckland
Mexico City ~ New Delhi ~ Hong Kong

First published by Scholastic Ltd, 1998

ISBN 0 590 54391 1

Printed by Cox and Wyman Ltd, Reading, Berks.

2 4 6 8 10 9 7 5 3 1

In a far-off Eastern land, a long, long time ago, there once lived a great and mighty Sultan. He was, without doubt, the richest, laziest, greediest and fattest Sultan there had ever been. He was so rich his palace was built of nothing but shining marble and glowing gold, so rich that even

the buttons on his silken clothes were made of diamonds. He was so lazy he had to have a special servant to brush his teeth for him, and another one to wash him, and another one to dress him.

He did nothing for himself, except eat. He was so greedy that every meal – breakfast, lunch and dinner – he'd gobble down a nice plump peacock just to himself, and a great bowl of sweetmeats, too. And then he'd wash it all down with a jug of honeyed camel's milk.

It was because he was so very lazy

and so very greedy that he was so very, very fat. He had to sleep in a bed wide enough for five grown men, and his pantaloons were the baggiest, most capacious pantaloons ever made for anyone anywhere.

But believe it or not there was something the Sultan cared about even more than his food — his treasure. He loved his treasure above anything else in the whole world.

Before he went to sleep every night, he would always open his treasure chest and count out his jewels — emeralds, rubies, diamonds, pearls,

sapphires, hundreds and hundreds of them – just to be quite sure they were all still there. Only then could he go to bed happy and sleep soundly.

But outside the walls of his palace, the Sultan's people lived like slaves, poor, wretched and hungry. They had to work every hour God gave them. And why? To keep the Sultan rich in jewels. Everything they harvested – their corn, their grapes, their figs, their dates, their pomegranates – all had to be given to the Sultan. He allowed them just enough food to keep body and soul together – no more.

One fine morning, the Sultan was out hunting. He loved to hunt, because all he had to do was sit astride his horse and send the hawks off to do the hunting. There was only one horse in the land strong enough to carry him, a great stout old warhorse. But strong though he was, to be sat on by the great fat Sultan for hour after hour under the hot, hot sun, proved too much even for him.

Lathered up and exhausted, the old warhorse staggered suddenly and stumbled, throwing the Sultan to the ground. It took ten servants to get him to his feet and brush him down. He wasn't badly hurt, just a bit bumped and bruised, but he was angry; very angry. He ordered his servants to whip the old horse soundly, so that he wouldn't do it again. Then they all helped him back up on his horse, which took some time, of course; and off they went back to the palace.

The Sultan didn't know it, not yet, and no more did anyone else, but he'd left something behind lying in the dirt on the dusty farmyard track, something that had popped off his waistcoat when he'd fallen from his horse. It was a button, a shining, glittering diamond button.

Just a little way off, down the farmyard track, was a tumbledown farmhouse

where there lived a poor old woman. She had little enough in this world — though she never complained of it — only a couple of nanny goats for her milk, a few hens for her eggs, *and* a little red rooster. She always kept the goats hidden away inside her house, and the hens too, for fear that the Sultan's servants might come by and steal them away for the Sultan.

She had always tried to keep her little red rooster in the house too, because she loved him dearly, and because she wanted him to keep her hens happy. But this was a little red

rooster with a mind of his own, and whenever he could, he would go running off to explore the big, wide world outside, to find friends — and to find food, for he was always very hungry.

That same day, when the poor old woman went out to fetch water for her goats and hens, the little red rooster scooted out from under her skirts. Before she could stop him he was out

through the open door and running off down the farm track.

"Come back, Little Red Rooster!" cried the poor old woman. "Come back! If the Sultan finds you, he'll catch you and eat you up. Come back!"

But the little red rooster had never in his life been frightened of anything or anyone. He just kept on running. "Catch me if you can, mistress mine," he called out.

On and on he ran, until he came to the farm track where the cornfield and the vineyard met. He knew this

was just the perfect place to scratch around for a good meal. Here he'd find all the ripe corn and dried-up sultanas he could eat. As he pecked about busily in the earth, he came across dozens of wriggling worms and singing cicadas and burrowing beetles, but he never ate these. After all, these were his friends. He couldn't eat his friends — though he had thought about it once or twice.

Meanwhile, back in his gold and marble palace, the great Sultan was stamping up and down. He was in a horrible temper, his stomachs and his chins wobbling with fury.

"The diamond button off my waistcoat," he roared. "I have lost my diamond button. Search, you miserable beggars, search everywhere, every nook and cranny." His servants were scurrying here and there and everywhere, all over the palace, but they could not find it anywhere.

"I'll lop off your heads if you don't find it," he bellowed. But no matter

how loud he shouted, how terrible the threats, no one could find the missing diamond button.

"Am I surrounded by nothing but fools and imbeciles?" he thundered. "I see I shall have to find it for myself. We shall go back and search every inch of the ground we hunted over this morning. And you will go in front of me, all of you on your knees in the dust where you belong, and search for my diamond button. Fetch me my horse." He clapped his hands. "At once. At once."

Out in the countryside, the little red rooster was scratching around in the dusty farm track at the edge of the cornfield. He scratched and he scratched. Suddenly there was something strange in the earth, something different, something very pretty that glistened and shone and twinkled in the sun. He tried eating it, but it didn't taste very good. So he dropped it. And then he had a sudden and

brilliant idea.

"I know," he said to himself. "Poor old mistress mine loves pretty things. She's always saying so, and she's got nothing pretty of her own. I'll take it home for her. Then she won't be cross with me for running away, will she?"

But just as he picked it up again, along the farm track came the great fat Sultan on his horse, and in front of him, dozens of his servants, all of them crawling on their hands and knees in the dirt. Closer and closer they came. All at once they spotted the little red rooster *and* the diamond

button too, glinting in his beak.

"There, my lord Sultan!" they cried. "Look! That little red rooster. He's got your diamond button."

"So that's what it is," the little red rooster said to himself.

The great fat Sultan rode up, scattering his servants hither and thither as he came. "Little Red Rooster," he said from high up on his horse. "I see you have my diamond button. I am your great and mighty Sultan. Give it to me at once. It's valuable, very valuable. And it's mine."

"I don't think so, Mr Sultana,"

replied the little red rooster, who had never in his life been frightened of anyone or anything. "Cockadoodledoo, Mr Sultana. Finders keepers. If it's so valuable, then I'm going to give it to poor old mistress mine. She needs it a lot more than you, I think. Sorry, Mr Sultana."

"What!" spluttered the Sultan. "Mr Sultana? How dare you speak to me like that? How dare you? Did you hear what that infernal bird called me? Fetch me that rooster. Fetch me my diamond button! Grab him! Grab that rooster!"

There was a frightful kerfuffle of dust and feathers and squawking, as the Sultan's servants tried to grab the little red rooster. Whatever they did, they just could not catch him. In the end, the little red rooster ran off into the cornfield. But although he'd escaped their clutches, he was very cross with himself, for in all the ker-fuffle he had dropped the diamond button.

One of the Sultan's servants found it lying in the dust and brought it back to the Sultan. The Sultan was delighted, of course, and all his servants were mightily relieved, too. Now, at least, none of them would have his head lopped off, not that day anyway.

But had the Sultan seen the last of the little red rooster? Not by any means. The little red rooster wasn't going to give up that easily – he wasn't like that. He followed the Sultan and his servants back to the palace. Then, in the middle of the night, as everyone slept, he flew up to

the Sultan's window, perched on the window-ledge, took a deep breath and crowed, and crowed. He let out the loudest, longest cockadoodle-doo he'd ever doodled in all his life.

"Cockadoodle-doo, Mr Sultana," he crowed. "Cockadoodle-doo!"

The Sultan tried to cover his ears. It didn't work.

"Cockadoodle-doo, Mr Sultana!"

The Sultan tried to bury his head in his pillow. It didn't work.

"Cockadoodle-doo, Mr Sultana! Give me back my diamond button."

By now the Sultan was in a terrible

rage. He had had quite enough of this. He called in his servants. "Grab me that infernal bird," he cried. "I know what I'll do. I know. We'll throw him in the well and drown him. That should shut him up, and shut him up for good."

All night long, the Sultan and his servants chased around the palace after the little red rooster. The little red

rooster had lots of fun. He played hide-and-seek behind the peacocks. He flew, he hopped, he ran. He perched on cornices, on chandeliers, on the Sultan's throne itself! And that was where they finally caught him. One of the servants crept up behind and grabbed him by his tail feathers.

The little red rooster didn't really mind – he'd had enough of the game anyway. He wasn't at all frightened of water. He knew what to do with water. He wasn't worried.

"Aha!" cried the exultant Sultan. "We've got you now. You've crowed your very last doodle-doo."

"I don't think so, Mr Sultana," said the little red rooster. But the Sultan took him by the neck and dropped him down the well. It was a long flutter down, and of course it was a bit wet when he landed. But the little red rooster didn't mind. He simply said to himself: "Come, my empty stomach. Come, my empty stomach and drink up all the water."

It took a bit of time, but that's just what he did. He drank up all the water, every last drop of it. Up and out of the well he flew, up and away, until he reached the Sultan's window.

"Cockadoodle-doo, Mr Sultana!" he cried. "Give me back my diamond button."

The Sultan could not believe his eyes. He could not believe his ears. "What!" he spluttered. "You again!" He called his servants. "Look!" he shrieked. "Can't you see? That infernal bird is back. I know what I'll do. I know. We'll grab him and throw him

into the fire. Let him burn." So the Sultan's servants rushed at the little red rooster and caught him.

"Aha!" cried the exultant Sultan. "We've got you now. You've crowed your very last doodle-doo."

"I don't think so, Mr Sultana," said the little red rooster. But the Sultan took him by the neck and threw him on the fire. He wasn't at all frightened of fire. He knew what to do with fire. He wasn't worried. He simply said to himself: "Come, my full-up stomach. Come, my full-up stomach, let out all the water and

put out all the fire."

It took a bit of time, but that's just what he did. He gushed out all the water and put out all the fire, every last spark of it. And up he flew again to the Sultan's window.

"Cockadoodle-doo, Mr Sultana," he cried. "Give me back my diamond button."

"What!" spluttered the Sultan.

"You again!"

Now the Sultan was really mad. He was beside himself with fury. He called his servants again. "Look! That infernal bird is back. I know what I'll do this time. I know. We'll grab him and throw him into the beehive. Let the bees sting him." And the Sultan's servants rushed at the little red rooster and caught him.

"Aha!" cried the exultant Sultan. "We've got you now. You've crowed your very last doodle-doo."

"I don't think so, Mr Sultana," said the little red rooster. But the

Sultan took him by the neck and threw him into the beehive. The little red rooster wasn't at all frightened by the bees. He knew what to do with bees. He wasn't worried. As the bees buzzed angrily all around him he simply said to himself: "Come, my empty stomach. Come, my empty stomach and eat up all the bees."

And that's just what he did. He ate up all the bees, every last one of them.

Back in the palace, the Sultan was rubbing his hands with glee. He thought for sure he had seen the last of the little red rooster. But he hadn't, had he?

He was happily tucking into his lunch of roast peacock, when suddenly he heard this: "Cockadoodle-doo, Mr Sultana! Give me back my diamond button." The little red rooster was back on the window-ledge.

"What!" spluttered the Sultan, his mouth full of peacock. "You again!"

Like a crazed camel, he was, like a vengeful vulture, like a gibbering

jackal. He stamped and stormed about the palace, shouting and screaming at his servants.

"Who will rid me of this infernal bird?" he cried. "Tell me. Tell me how to do it, or I'll lop off your heads. I will! I will!"

And the servants knew he meant it, too. So naturally they all thought about how they could get rid of the little red rooster. They thought very hard, very hard indeed.

"Hang him by the neck from the pomegranate tree, my lord Sultan," said one. But the Sultan shook his head.

"Lop off his head, my lord Sultan," said another.

"It's no good," wailed the Sultan. "He'd only run around without it." And he sat down in deep despair on his cushions.

But then, just as he was sitting down, he heard the cushions sighing and groaning underneath him. He was squashing them flat! "That's it!" he cried, leaping to his feet. "I know what I'll do. I know. Grab me that infernal bird. I'll sit on him and flatten him. I'll squash him. I'll squish him. I'll obsquatulate him!" From the

window-ledge the little red rooster heard it all and smiled inside himself.

The Sultan's servants rushed at the little red rooster and caught him.

"Aha!" cried the exultant Sultan. "We've got you now. You've crowed your very last doodle-doo."

"I don't think so, Mr Sultana," said the little red rooster. But the Sultan took the little red rooster by the neck, stuffed him down the back of his pantaloons and then sat down on him hard, very hard indeed.

The little red rooster wasn't at all frightened of being obsquatulated.

He knew what to do about that. He wasn't worried. He simply said to himself: "Come, my full-up stomach. Come, my full-up stomach, let out all the bees and sting the Sultan's bottom."

And were those bees angry? I should say so. And did they all sting the great and mighty Sultan's bottom? I should say so. There was plenty of room in those capacious pantaloons for every bee to sting wherever he wanted. And remember, that great and mighty Sultan had a very large, very round bottom, probably the

biggest bottom the world had ever seen!

Did the great fat Sultan jump up and down? I should say so. Did he screech and yowl and whimper? I should say so. And did the little red rooster hop out of those great pantaloons and fly off safe and sound? Of course he did.

"Aiee! Ow! Youch! Oosh, oosh, ooh!" cried the Sultan, as he sat with his stinging bottom dunked in a bath of ice-cold water.

"Cockadoodle-doo, Mr Sultana!" cried the little red rooster. "Now, will

you let me have back my diamond
button?"

"All right, all right," said the
Sultan. "I give in. Anything, anything
to get you out of my sight. Take him
up to my room and give him his con-
founded diamond button. It's in my
treasure chest."

So the Sultan's servants took the
little red rooster up to the Sultan's
bedchamber, and gave him the diamond button from out of the Sultan's
treasure chest.

"Now go," they cried. "Fly away!
Shoo! You've got what you came for.

Go, before you get us into any more trouble."

"I'm going. I'm going," replied the little red rooster, the diamond button in his beak. But he was in no hurry to go, for something had caught his eye. He could not believe his luck. The Sultan's treasure chest! The servants had left it open! So he flew away only as far as the window-ledge, and he waited there till all the servants had left. Then he flew down and hopped across the room and up on to the treasure chest. Emeralds, rubies, diamonds, pearls, sapphires — the finest jewels in

the entire world.

"Ah well. In for a penny, in for a pound," said the little red rooster to himself. "Come, my empty stomach. Come, my empty stomach and gobble down the Sultan's jewels."

And that's just what he did. He gobbled down all the Sultan's jewels, every last one of them.

Then out he flew, out of the window and out over the palace walls, which was not at all easy, because he was rather heavy by now. He had to waddle all the rest of the way back home, rattling as he went.

As he neared the farm, he happened to meet up with his friends again, the wriggling worms and the singing cicadas and the burrowing beetles. So, of course, he just had to tell them all about his great adventures in the Sultan's palace. He was only halfway through his story when the poor old woman, who had been looking high and low for him, spied him at last. She came scuttling along the farm track.

"Where have you been, Little Red Rooster?" she cried. "I've been worried sick."

"Ah, mistress mine," replied the little red rooster. "Never in your life will you ever have to worry again. And never will we have to go hungry again, either. Look what I have for you."

And he said to himself: "Come, my full-up stomach. Come, my full-up stomach and give up all your jewels."

Out they poured on to the ground, all of them, all the Sultan's jewels, until there was a great sparkling pile

of them at the poor old woman's feet. Only, she wasn't poor any more, was she?

It took the breath right out of her. She sat down with a bump, still trying to believe her eyes.

"Goodness me!" she cried. "Goodness me!"

And she *was* good too, goodness itself. Do you know what she did? She gave those jewels to all her poor friends in

the countryside round about, just enough for each of them so that no one had too much. She kept for herself all she needed, and no more. But, of course, the little red rooster got to keep his diamond button.

Just you try and take it from him!

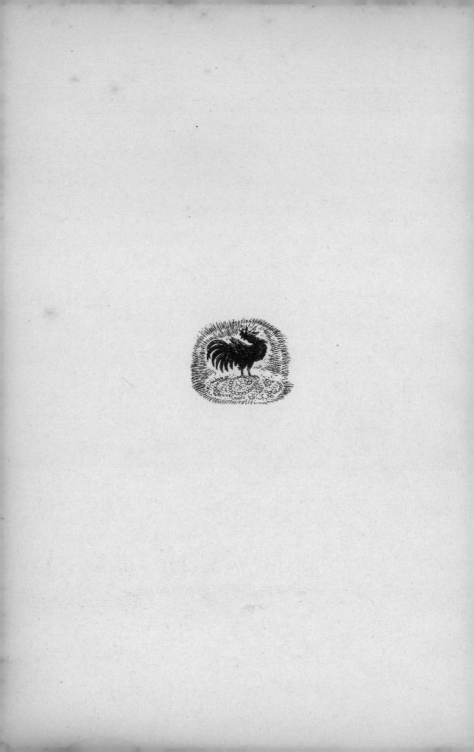